Mr

Icy-Cold

and

Other Stories

by

ENID BLYTON

Illustrated by
Maureen Bradley

AWARD PUBLICATIONS

ISBN 0-86163-588-4

Text copyright 1948 Darrell Waters Limited
Illustrations copyright © 1993 Award Publications Limited

Enid Blyton's signature is a trademark of Darrell Waters Limited

First published 1948 by Basil Blackwell

This edition entitled *Mr Icy-Cold and Other Stories*
First published 1993

Published by Award Publications Limited,
The Old Riding School, Welbeck Estate, Nr. Worksop, Notts.

Printed in Hungary

CONTENTS

Mr Icy-Cold

Once upon a time, one very snowy week, six children began to build a snowman. How hard they worked! You should have seen them, scraping the snow off the grass and off the top of the hedges, slapping it together to make the snowman's body, and patting it neatly into shape.

"This is fun!" said Mary.

"He will be the biggest snowman ever seen!" said Alan.

"I shall ask Mother to give me an old cap of Daddy's for him to wear," said Rachel.

"Let's give him two feet, and put shoes on them so that he can walk about if he wants to!" said John.

The others laughed. "I *should* be

5

astonished if I saw him walking down the garden!" said Ian.

"We'll call him Mr Icy-Cold!" said Gillian.

When they had finished the snowman it was three o'clock. "Now we will dress him!" said Mary.

"He has a head as big as a giant's football!" said Alan.

"Here's Daddy's old cap for him!" said Rachel, running up with a big checked cap and putting it on the snowman's head. He did look splendid!

"And here are two old shoes belonging to Grandpa!" said John, putting them on the snowman's feet. It was difficult to put them on! John filled the shoes with snow, and then pushed them well under the snowman, so that they stuck out in a very realistic manner!

"He's going to walk, he's going to walk!" cried Ian.

"Come along indoors and have a nice hot drink of milk, Mr Icy-Cold!" shouted Gillian.

"He wouldn't like that," said Mother, coming up to look at the wonderful snowman. "It would melt him inside!"

The children went in to tea. When the moon rose up in the sky, just about their bedtime, they looked out of the window and saw Mr Icy-Cold standing out there in the garden looking as real as could be. He wore Daddy's cap, he had an old pipe in his mouth, he had two great black eyes, he wore a ragged scarf round his neck, old gloves on his hands, and Grandpa's shoes. He really looked marvellous.

In the middle of the night a crowd of little snow-elves came flying up in their pretty sleigh, drawn by winter moths. When they saw Mr Icy-Cold they flew down to him at once.

"Oh!" they cried. "A great big snowman! What is your name, Snowman?"

"I am Mr Icy-Cold," said the snowman, in a soft snowy sort of voice. "Come and talk to me."

The snow-elves told him where they had come from – a land far away to the north, where there was always ice, always frost, always snow. The elves were pretty little creatures with frosty dresses, and wings as soft and as white

8

as snow. Mr Icy-Cold liked them very much indeed. He felt lonely when they had gone. But they promised to come again the next night.

They kept their promise – but to Mr Icy-Cold's great dismay they were crying bitterly!

"What's the matter?" asked Mr Icy-Cold.

"Oh, two naughty pixies chased us, and broke our pretty sleigh. Look! It's no use now! We can't use it any more. We don't know what to do because when the weather turns warm, we must fly away to our own country of ice and snow. If we stay here when it is warm, we feel ill and fade away."

Mr Icy-Cold was very sorry to hear all this.

"Where do those two pixies live?" he asked. "I will go to them and make them mend your sleigh for you, or else give you a new one."

"But snowmen can't walk!" cried the snow-elves.

"Oh, *can't* they!" said Mr Icy-Cold, and he laughed. "Look!"

He stepped forward on his two big feet, and the elves cried out in surprise, for they had never seen a snowman walk before. He plodded down the garden and back, his two big shoes leaving footprints behind him.

"There you are!" he said. "What did I tell you? Now where do those two naughty pixies live? I'll go and give them the fright of their lives!"

"Come with us and we'll show you," said the elves, and dragging their broken sleigh behind them, they took the snowman down the garden, through a gate at the bottom, and into a field. The field sloped up into a hill, and in the middle of the hill was a little door.

"This is where the pixies live," said the elves, half-frightened. Mr Icy-Cold knocked at the door softly. As soon as

it was opened by the two pixies, the snowman reached out his big gloved hand and caught hold of them.

"Oooh! Ow! Oooh!" yelled the pixies, in a fright. "Here's a big white giant! Oooh! Let us go!"

"You broke the sleigh belonging to the snow-elves!" said the snowman sternly. "What are you going to do about it?"

"Oh, we'll mend it; oh, do let us go! We promise to mend it!" squealed the pixies. Mr Icy-Cold put them down on the ground, and looked at them sternly out of his big black stone-eyes.

11

"Do it at once, or I'll carry you off with me!" he said. The pixies took the broken sleigh and looked at it. One of them fetched hammer and nails and screws. The other brought a few pieces of wood. Soon the night air was filled with the sound of hammering. Every now and again the two pixies stared round in fear at the big snowman, and he frowned as hard as he could.

"Get on with your job!" he said. So they hurried and hurried. The wind blew chill and Jack Frost was out and about. The pixies were cold and wanted to get back into their warm little house. Soon the sleigh was mended, and the snow-elves got into it with glad shouts and cries.

"Don't you dare to interfere with the snow-elves again!" said Mr Icy-Cold, and off he shuffled back to his place in the garden. The snow-elves went with him, making a great fuss of him, and telling him he was their best friend.

After that the elves and the snowman talked together every night. But soon the weather changed and the air became warm. The snow-elves began to think about going back to their own country of ice and snow.

"But how lonely I shall be without you!" said Mr Icy-Cold sadly. "I shall stand here, thinking of you, all the spring and summer through, until the winter comes again and brings you with it."

"No, Mr Icy-Cold, you won't stay here all the spring and the summer," said the elves. "You will melt. You will melt right away, and there will be nothing of you left when we come back next winter."

Mr Icy-Cold stared at the elves in horror, and his stone eyes seemed to get bigger and bigger.

"Melt!" he said. "Did you say I shall melt? Won't there be anything left of me?"

"Not a thing," said the elves sadly. "That's the worst of being a snowman, you know. You only last whilst the snow and ice are here. Then you disappear for ever."

Nobody spoke for a minute. Mr Icy-Cold was too upset, and the elves too sad. Then a small elf gave a little squeal and made everybody jump.

"I've got an idea, I've got an idea!" she cried. "Why shouldn't Mr Icy-Cold come back to our land with us! It's always cold and frosty there, and snow is always on the ground. He would never melt there. He would be able to live with us for ever!"

"Of course, of course!" shouted the snow-elves in delight. "You must start tonight, Mr Icy-Cold. We will make our winter moths fly very slowly, and you

must follow us carefully. Come now, this very minute – for the weather is getting warmer, and if you begin to melt you may not be able to walk!"

So Mr Icy-Cold followed the little sleigh, drawn by moths, and plodded on and on and on towards the north. He went over fields and hills, down lanes and high roads, and the elves always found a good place to hide him in the daytime.

Once the weather got a bit too warm, and the snowman's nose melted a bit. But the next night was frosty again, so he was all right. And at last he got to the land of the snow-elves. He was safe!

"Welcome to our home!" cried the snow-elves, kissing him on his cold cheek. "You shall build yourself a little snowhouse with windows and a door, and do just whatever you like."

The six children who had built the snowman were most surprised to find him gone.

"Oh, he's just melted," said Mother.

"But, Mother, his cap, and his scarf, and his gloves and his shoes can't have melted too!" said Mary. "It's most mysterious! I wonder where he is, funny old Mr Icy-Cold?"

He was building himself a little house in the land of the snow-elves, as happy as could be! And there he lives to this day, still wearing the same old cap and the same old shoes – funny Mr Icy-Cold!

The
Left-Behind Cat

Tabby was a small striped cat with green eyes. She had a loud purr and a long tail. When she was pleased she rubbed her head against the nearest person and her tail stood up in the air.

Tabby belonged to Mrs Jones. She liked Mrs Jones because Mrs Jones had a nice warm fire in the kitchen, and every day she put down a plate of scraps and a saucer of milk for Tabby to eat and drink. Tabby liked Mr Jones too. He could scratch her very hard round the ears, and she loved that.

There were two Jones children, Amanda and John. They played with Tabby and rolled her over and gave her a cotton-reel on a bit of string. Tabby liked her home and the bit of garden where she basked in the sun. She was a happy little cat.

Now, when August came, the Jones family thought they would go to the seaside. What fun it would be to lie on the warm sand, to bathe, and dig, and eat ice-creams! Amanda and John were excited. Even Tabby got excited when she saw them packing up and rushing about to find all kinds of things they wanted to take away.

"What shall we do with Tabby whilst we are away?" asked Amanda suddenly. "Are we going to lock the house up, Mummy?"

"Oh yes," said Mummy. "All the doors and windows will be locked and bolted in case a burglar should come. Perhaps Mrs Brown will have Tabby for us."

But Mrs Brown was going away too, so she couldn't.

"We'll ask Mrs Thomas," said Mummy. But Mrs Thomas said no, she couldn't possibly have Tabby because she kept canaries.

"Can't we send her away to a place where people keep cats and dogs when their owners are away?" asked John. "Peter's dog went to a good place whilst his family were away."

"Oh, no, we can't send Tabby anywhere like that," said Mummy. "It is expensive. I'll think of something, don't worry."

But do you know, in all the hurry and bustle of packing, everyone forgot about Tabby! Mummy didn't ask anyone else – and at last the morning came when the Jones family were to go to the sea for two weeks.

Amanda remembered Tabby ten minutes before they started.

"Mummy, Mummy!" she called. "What about Tabby?"

Mrs Jones was hot and bothered and cross.

"Tabby will have to look after herself," she said. "She can easily catch mice and birds, and I'll get Mrs Terry next door to put down some milk each day. Now, don't worry me any more."

They all went off in a taxi, excited and happy. Mr Jones locked the front door and saw that every window was shut and fastened. He shut the front gate. Bang! He was gone.

Tabby was lying on top of the wall wondering what all the excitement was about. She watched the taxi out of sight. She wondered when the family would be back.

"They'll be back by tea-time, I'm sure," thought Tabby. "Mrs Jones always give me my milk then."

Tabby lazed in the sun. But soon the sun went in and dark clouds blew up. The rain poured down. Tabby didn't like her coat wet so she jumped down and ran to the back door. But the door was shut too.

"Oh, where can I go?" thought Tabby, in dismay. She ran in the rain to

the shed where the Jones family kept their bicycles. But will you believe it, that was shut too! Tabby crouched under a bush, licking the raindrops off her fur when they dripped through the leaves.

At tea-time the house was still shut. Mrs Jones was not there to give Tabby her meal. Tabby was very hungry. She wondered how she could get something to eat.

There were no mice about in the daytime. Indeed, there were very few mice at all, for no one left food about. Tabby would have liked a nice fat mouse, but she knew quite well it was no good hunting for one.

As for birds, they were much too clever! There were too many cats in the road for the birds to be tame. The stupid, foolish birds had been killed long ago. Only the quick sharp ones were left. Tabby knew she would never be able to catch one. She had often tried.

The little cat stayed under the bush

till the rain had stopped. Then, walking on tiptoes over the wet grass, she jumped up on the wall between her garden and the next. Perhaps Mrs Terry next door would give her something to eat.

But Mrs Terry didn't like Tabby. Tabby had once sat on some seeds she had planted, and she always drove her away whenever she saw her now. She caught sight of the little cat in her garden, and she rushed out and shooed her away.

"Off with you! Off with you!" she said. "You naughty little cat! I'm not going to have you prowling about my

23

garden now the Joneses have gone away! And you needn't think I'll give you any food either. If I do that, you'll think you can live in my garden, and spoil all my plants."

Tabby leapt back to her own garden again. The sun came out and she warmed herself. She thought she had better wait patiently till the family came home again. She felt sure they would be back that night.

But they didn't come back that night. No, they were far away, down by the sea. They would not be back until two weeks had passed. They were

happy – so happy that not one of them had thought of poor little Tabby!

Tabby slept under the damp bush. There was nowhere else to go. She had run to the sheds she knew in other gardens but they had all been shut but one – and that one already had a cat inside, who wouldn't let Tabby come in.

Just before dawn Tabby woke up, cold and hungry. She was so dreadfully hungry that she felt she *must* catch a mouse. So she crept quietly about, sniffing here and there. But there wasn't a single mouse anywhere!

All that day Tabby waited about for the Jones family to come back. She mewed outside the front door. She mewed outside the back door. She wanted her nice basket by the kitchen

fire. She wanted her dinner. She wanted some milk. She wanted a little petting and love.

But the Jones family still didn't come back. Tabby went hunting round the dustbins of the houses in the road. She found an old bone. She found a crust of bread. She drank water from a goldfish pond three gardens away until the dog came and chased her up to the wall.

Then she went back to her own garden and lay on the wall again. The big black cat that lived two doors away came and sat beside her.

"You look miserable," he said. "What's the matter?"

"My family has been away yesterday and today," said Tabby. "It is very strange. I can't get into the house. No one gave me any food, and I am so hungry."

"Your family has gone away for a long time," said the black cat, washing his face well with his wetted paw. "I heard my mistress say so."

"Why didn't they take me too?" cried Tabby.

"Cats never get taken away, like dogs," said the black cat. "They forgot all about you, I expect."

"Oh, they couldn't!" mewed Tabby. "Why, they love me, and I love them. I'm their cat!"

"Well, they can't love you very much if they go off and leave you without a home or food," said the black cat, washing behind his ears. "I should run away, if I were you. I wouldn't want to belong to such a horrid family."

"But I love them," said Tabby. "I do really. I can't believe they would do such a thing."

27

"You're just a silly, soft-hearted little tabby," said the black cat, getting up. "Well, I must go. I hope you don't starve. I can spare you a drink of milk now and then if you like – but beware of our dog. He doesn't mind me, but he hates strange cats."

The black cat ran back home. Tabby was left all alone. And now indeed she was dreadfully miserable. Could her family *really* have forgotten her? Didn't they think about her at all? Her whiskers drooped and she gave a small mew. She was a very sad little cat.

The days went on. Tabby caught a cold through sleeping out in the rain, for the weather was very wet just then. She couldn't find enough to eat – just

little scraps now and again. She grew thin, and her fur lost its lovely shine. Soon she had the scared, frightened, lean look of a stray cat that has no home or family.

One day she felt so ill that she could hardly crawl. She dragged herself to the front door and lay there, mewing faintly, though she knew quite well by now that there was no one to let her in.

Now down the road just then came a red-headed boy, whistling cheerily. His name was Sandy, and he had quick eyes and ears. He heard the faint mewing and stopped. He soon saw the little cat by the front door of the house, and he stared at it.

"I believe the poor little thing is

starving!" he said. "It's as thin as can be! This house is shut up – I wonder if the people went away and left their poor little cat behind, without food or shelter?"

He went in at the gate. He picked up the cat and put it under his coat. "I'll take you home to my mother," he said. "She'll know what to do. She never says no to anything hurt or ill."

He carried Tabby home. His mother was sorry to see her looking so ill and thin. "She is starving," said Sandy's mother. "And she has a dreadful cold too. Poor little thing! I should think someone has gone away and left her behind."

Sandy gave Tabby some hot milk. How she lapped it up! His mother found an old basket and put a bit of warm blanket inside. She lifted Tabby in and set her by the kitchen fire. "Although it's summertime, it's cold and wet this week," she said. "You want warmth, then you'll lose your cold."

For seven days Sandy nursed Tabby, and soon the little cat grew fat and her coat shone like silk again. She purred and rubbed her head against Sandy's legs. Sandy loved feeling her.

"Could we keep her, Mummy?" he asked. "If her family *did* leave her behind, uncared-for, they don't deserve to have her back."

"We'll ask the policeman if anyone has lost a cat, and if he doesn't know of anyone, we'll keep her," said Mummy. "She really is a darling."

31

The policeman didn't know of anyone who had lost a cat – so Tabby had a new home and a new family, one that would never, never go away and leave her behind without food or friends.

When the Jones family came back, they opened the house and unpacked. Then they looked for Tabby. But she wasn't there.

"Tabby, Tabby, Tabby!" called Amanda. But no Tabby came. Amanda burst into tears. "Where is she?" she sobbed. "I want her."

But Tabby didn't come back, though Amanda and John called her a hundred times the next day. Mrs Terry looked at them over the fence.

"Do stop shouting for that cat of yours," she said. "I saw it a week ago, looking really ill and so thin it was like a shadow. I should think it is dead. It serves you right for going away and forgetting about it, poor creature. I don't like cats myself, but I wouldn't treat one like that if I kept one."

Amanda and John cried themselves to sleep that night, and were very unhappy. They didn't know that Tabby was alive and well and happy two streets away, with a new family that she loved! But I don't feel very sorry for the Jones family, do you? They deserved to lose their little Tabby-cat.

Chinky Goes Adventuring

Chinky was a big, strong brownie who lived in a fine cottage in the middle of Pitpat Village. He had a little servant, a gnome called Dimity, a quiet fellow with a nice smile and neat ways. Dimity thought Chinky a fine brownie and waited on him all day long.

Now Chinky had great ideas of himself. He felt that he had the makings of a hero. If only something would happen so that he could show all the village folk how brave, how full of courage and plucky he was!

"You know, Dimity," Chinky sometimes said, "if a house caught on fire, I'd be the first one to go and save all the people in it!"

"I'm sure you would, Chinky," said

Dimity admiringly.

"And if a horse ran away I'd be the first one to stop him!" said Chinky.

"There's no doubt about that!" said Dimity, gazing in admiration at tall, strong Chinky.

"And if someone fell into the pond and couldn't swim I'd jump in straight away and pull him out!" boasted Chinky.

"But I thought you couldn't swim," said Dimity.

"Oh, that wouldn't matter!" said Chinky. "I'd be brave enough to jump in all the same."

"You are so big and strong, Chinky,"

said Dimity, with a sigh. "I'm such a little fellow, and not brave at all. Why, I even run when I see a big spider!"

"You are weak and foolish, Dimity," said Chinky grandly. "Never mind – you have a brave master. If only I could show what a fine fellow I am! Nobody seems to think I am anything out of the ordinary. I never have any adventures."

It was true. Pitpat Village was quiet and well-behaved. No one did anything they shouldn't. Nobody ever had a house on fire. None of the horses ever ran away. Nobody ever fell into the pond or the stream. There were no adventures to be had at all.

So no one knew that Chinky felt so brave. They just nodded to him when

they met him, and said "Good-day!" Or they asked him out to tea and showed him their fine roses or their best sweet-peas and their biggest marrows. It seemed very dull to big, brave Chinky.

"Dimity," said Chinky, at last, "I am going to seek adventures. Pack up your things and we will set out tomorrow. If adventures will not come to me, I must go to them."

So Dimity packed their things into one big bag, put it on his shoulder and they set out. Chinky had long, strong legs and he got along fast. Dimity was always out of breath, for his legs were thin and small, and he had to carry the heavy bag. So he always seemed to be running to catch up with Chinky!

They walked and they walked. They passed right through Pitpat Village and Chinky shouted to everyone how he was going on brave adventures, and they nodded in surprise.

"You will do something one day, Chinky!" they called, and Chinky marched on, pleased. He left the village behind. He came to farmland, and walked over fields and meadows. And then he came to his first adventure!

"Look!" he cried, stopping and pointing. "There is something on fire!"

Dimity looked. Yes – smoke was rising up from behind a hedge, and flames crackled loudly.

"It must be a shed or something," said Chinky. "Hurry, Dimity, and get a pail for me. There is a stream here, and

I will put out the fire. I knew I could be a hero if I had the chance!"

Dimity rushed to a barn not far off, found a pail, and took it to Chinky. Chinky filled it with water from the stream and threw it on the flames – and yet more. Soon the fire sizzled loudly, and a cloud of black smoke rose into the air instead of flames and blue smoke.

"The fire is going out," said Chinky. "I have put it out!"

Just at that moment there came a roar from behind him. Chinky turned and saw a farmer standing there looking very angry indeed.

"What have you done to my bonfire?" he shouted. "I was burning up all my rubbish – and now you have interfered and put out the fire! How dare you!"

Chinky stared at the angry farmer and then at the fire. Yes – it was a bonfire. He could see that quite plainly now. The farmer lifted up his stick and ran towards Chinky – and the brownie ran away in terrible fright! Over the fields he ran, and up the hill and down, and he didn't stop until he had lost all

his breath. Dimity panted behind him.

Chinky said nothing at all. He didn't feel very brave. Soon he got up and went on again, and it wasn't long before he found his next adventure!

"Look!" he said to Dimity. "Someone has left their shopping basket behind! They must have put it down for a moment and then forgotten it. We will find the owner – and how pleased she will be!"

Dimity saw the basket by the hedge, full of bags and parcels. Yes – someone had been shopping – but who? There was no one in sight.

"Shall I carry the basket, Chinky?" Dimity asked.

"Oh, no, I'll carry it," said Chinky, who was longing to see the owner and have her thanks. He picked it up and set off with it. But he hadn't gone very far before there came an angry yell from the other side of the hedge.

"Stop thief! Stop thief! He's got my basket! I just stepped through the hedge to say good morning to Mrs Flip

and someone came along and took my basket! There's the thief! Stop thief! Stop thief!"

A big fat brownie woman came running down the path, red in the face, looking as angry as could be. Behind her came another brownie woman, carrying a rolling-pin.

"Excuse me, madam," began Chinky politely – but the brownie women did not listen to him. One smacked him on the cheek and the other hit him on the shoulder with her rolling-pin. Poor Chinky! He dropped the basket and fled down the path as fast as ever he could, crying tears all down his nice new coat! He was dreadfully frightened.

Dimity followed with the big bag, panting and puffing, very sorry for his master.

42

Chinky dried his tears and went on his way. He felt brave again, ready to go in for any adventure that came, but he did not mean to put out fires nor to pick up baskets. No – he wanted something grander than that!

And he soon found it! He came to a river and saw, in the middle, a boat, rowed by a magician. Sitting in the boat were four pixie-like creatures, with no wings. Just as the boat floated opposite, the magician stopped rowing, took hold of the first pixie and threw him into the water!

"One!" he said. Then he took the second and threw him in as well, "Two!" Then the third – "Three!" And then the last. "Four!" shouted the magician, and stood up in his boat shouting in excitement.

"Look!" said Chinky to Dimity, throwing off his coat. "Four poor little pixies thrown into the water by that wicked magician! I must rescue them!"

"But you can't swim!" wailed Dimity. Chinky took no notice. He dived into the water and tried to wade out to the pixies – but the water was deep, and, as Dimity had said, Chinky could not swim! So he began to flounder about and shout for help at the top of his voice.

The four pixies, who had been swimming very strongly to the opposite bank, turned at once and made their

way to the struggling brownie. They surrounded him and took him to the boat. The magician pulled him in and gazed angrily at him.

"What do you want to get into deep water like this for when you can't swim?" he said. "I put my four pixies in to have a race, and you have spoilt it all. Silly, interfering creature! I shall take you back with me and make you my servant! Spoiling my plans like this!"

Chinky was dreadfully frightened. He didn't say a word.

He didn't like to tell the magician that he had thought he was cruel and had thrown the pixies into the water to drown them. He sat in the boat, shivering and trembling.

Dimity was on the bank, in a terrible way, wondering what was going to happen to Chinky. As the boat was rowed along, he followed it, running on the path. Soon the boat pulled up at a landing-stage, and Dimity saw the magician take hold of poor Chinky very

roughly, and haul him up a path and into his house. The four pixies followed. The door slammed. Chinky was a prisoner!

Dimity sat down in dismay. He was very much afraid of magicians. But somehow or other Chinky had got to be rescued. He waited until night had come and everything was dark. Then he crept round to the back of the house and looked in at the window. There, sitting in a corner, with his hands tied, he saw Chinky. No one was with him. Good!

Dimity broke the window with a stone, jumped inside, cut the cords that bound Chinky's hands, and pulled him

46

to the window. At that moment the magician came running in – but Dimity picked up a chair and threw it at him. The magician fell over and yelled in surprise. Before he had picked himself up Chinky and Dimity had disappeared into the night!

And it wasn't *very* long before the two of them were sitting safely and comfortably at home, drinking hot cocoa and grinning shyly at one another. Chinky looked rather red.

"Dimity," he said, "I have been foolish. I have found that I am not a hero after all. I don't want to be one, either. I want to stay happily at home with you. But you, Dimity, you are a *real* hero! When I was caught and tied up by the magician, you rescued me, though you must have been very much afraid. You are a brave fellow, Dimity, full of courage. I am proud to have you for a friend – not a servant any more, Dimity, but a friend!"

Dimity was too happy to speak at first. Then he hugged Chinky and smiled. "I'm not a hero!" he said. "I don't want to be one, either. But I love you, Chinky, and so I was brave. But I am not brave really!"

So they had no more adventures, which was just as well, and lived happily together in Pitpat Village – and, unless they have moved, they are still there, to this very day!

The
Noah's Ark Lion

Katie had a big Noah's ark. It was a lovely one, and besides the Noah family, there were two of every animal you could think of! Lions, tigers, bears, horses, goats, dogs, giraffes, elephants, ducks, turkeys, pigs – there didn't seem to be any animal that wasn't there!

Katie had a lovely time playing with them each day. She set them out in twos and made them walk into the ark with Mr and Mrs Noah. They liked this very much.

But at night the Noah's ark animals had even better fun! Mr Noah opened the door of the ark and let them all out to play! My goodness me, what fun they had then!

They all tumbled out on to the ground and played whatever game they liked best. The ducks and the hens played hide-and-seek, the giraffes and the elephants played touch-me-last, and the white and brown bears played kiss-in-the-ring. Mr and Mrs Noah, and Shem, Ham and Japheth, their wooden children, watched them and laughed.

When it was time for all the animals to go back into the ark they were lined up in twos and marched in quietly. Then Mr Noah shut the door after them and they all lay quietly in the ark without moving, waiting for the time to come when Katie would open the lid and take them out.

Now all the animals were very good except the lion. He thought a great deal of himself ever since he had heard Katie call him the king of the beasts.

50

He wandered off each night by himself, for he thought he was too grand to play games with the others. He sat by the fire and curled his long tail round him. Sometimes he nibbled a bit of the hearth-rug. Sometimes he climbed up to the clock on the bookshelf and listened to its funny, ticking voice.

And when he heard Mr Noah calling all the animals back into the ark, the lion turned up his brown nose and stayed where he was! He didn't want to go into the ark. Wasn't he the king of all the beasts? Why should he be hustled into the ark like the stupid ducks and hens and pigs?

Mr Noah got so cross with the lion.

"Where's that lion tonight?" he would say. "He is just too tiresome for anything! Lion, lion, come at once! The

51

twos are all ready to march into the ark, and your lioness is waiting. Come at once."

But usually Shem had to go and find him and drag him to the ark. It was a great nuisance because it kept all the other animals waiting.

Now this happened night after night, and Mr Noah got very tired of it.

"If you don't come when you're called tonight, lion, we shall march into the ark without you, and you will be shut out!" he said firmly.

"They won't dare to go without me," thought the lion to himself. "I shall keep them waiting as long as I please! Am I not the king of them all?"

That night he sat himself down by the warm fire, curled his tail round him like a cat, and looked down his nose at the bears playing kiss-in-the-ring nearby.

When the time came, Mr Noah called to the animals. "Come to the ark! Line up in twos! It is time to go back."

All the animals and birds at once stopped their play and ran to the ark. The kangaroos were first. They stood at the head, and after them came the white bears, and then the brown bears, and then the ducks, and then the giraffes, and then, all by herself, the lioness. The lion was missing as usual. The line stretched out in twos, and ended with the elephants, who had been playing hide-and-seek, and had

had to scramble out of the coal-scuttle to get to the ark.

Mr Noah saw that the lion was missing. But he said nothing. He didn't even look round to see where the lion was. He didn't tell Shem to go and get him. He just said, "Shem, open the door. Ham, see that the elephants don't tread on the pigs, Japheth, tell the dogs to stop barking. Mrs Noah, would you be good enough to lead the way in?"

Mrs Noah led the way. The animals went in two by two, except the lioness, who went in by herself. Ham scolded the elephants because they trod on the pigs' tails.

Mr Noah went in last. He shut the door with a bang. Everyone settled down in the ark. Not a sound was to be heard.

Now the lion was rather astonished to see that all the animals had gone in without him. But he didn't say a word or even move from the hearth-rug where he sat warming himself.

"I shall stay out as long as I like," he said to himself grandly. He looked round and saw that all the other toys were going into the toy-cupboard. The soldier and the dolls and the teddy-bear always came out to play at night, too. But now they were settling down quietly.

The soldier was surprised to see the lion on the hearth-rug. "Aren't you going to get into the ark?" he asked. "Won't you be frightened out here all alone?"

"Frightened!" said the lion, turning up his nose. "Me frightened! Don't you know I am the king of all the beasts, and as brave as can be? What should frighten *me* I should like to know?"

"Well, if you feel as grand as all that, you can do what you like!" said the soldier, in a huff. "I'm sure I don't care, Mr High-and-Mighty!"

He got into the toy-cupboard and

slammed the door. The lion was now all alone. He sat on the rug and blinked at the fire. There was hardly any red coal left. It would soon be out. The nursery was dark, but the lion could see quite well. He had eyes like a cat.

He sat there, and he sat there. Suddenly he heard a scratching noise in the wall nearby. He jumped to his feet. Whatever could it be?

It was the little brown mouse who lived behind the wall. He was coming out of his hole to see if the children had left any crumbs on the floor. He sidled out of the hole and ran over the hearth-rug. He bumped into the lion and knocked him over.

"Don't!" said the lion. The mouse stared at him and grinned. He ran at the lion and knocked him over again.

"I said 'Don't!'" said the lion, in his grandest voice. "Well, you're sitting on a crumb," said the mouse. "Get off it. I want to eat it."

The lion sat down on the crumb and

wouldn't move. He felt very angry with the mouse.

"I wonder if *you* are good to eat!" said the mouse suddenly. "Do you mind if I nibble you tail?"

"Yes, I do mind," said the lion, scared. The mouse tried to get the lion's tail in his mouth and the lion ran away. The mouse chased him. Aha! This was fun!

"I'll get your tail!" squeaked the mouse. "I'll get it!"

The lion ran to the ark and knocked at the door. "Let me in! A mouse is chasing me."

"The door is locked," said Mr Noah. "Do not wake us up."

The lion ran to the toy-cupboard, and knocked there. "Let me in!" he cried. "A mouse is chasing me!"

"Go away," said the soldier sleepily. "Do not wake us."

Well, the lion would certainly have had his tail nibbled if someone hadn't come into the nursery on velvet paws, and scared the mouse away. And that someone was the big tabby cat! She had smelt the mouse and had come after him.

The mouse shot into his hole. The cat saw the lion running and thought he must be a mouse too. So she went after him, and at last she caught him. She pushed him over and sniffed at him. He was very frightened. He felt sure she would eat him.

"You smell strange," said the cat. "Very strange. You smell of wood and paint. I will not eat you – but I will play with you."

She began to push the poor lion about and throw him up into the air. He ran away as fast as he could and once more banged at the door of the ark.

"Let me in, let me in!" he cried. "A cat is after me."

"The door is locked," said Mr Noah. "Do not wake us up."

Then the lion ran to the toy-cupboard and knocked there again. "Let me in!" he cried. "A cat is after me."

"Go away," said the soldier sleepily. "Do not wake us."

The poor lion was quite in despair – and then he suddenly saw the cat running out of the door. She had heard a mouse downstairs! She was gone.

The lion sat down in front of the fire again, tired and miserable. How he wished he was safely in the ark with all the others! As he sat there a big spider ran over the rug and made him jump!

"Whatever's this now!" cried the lion. "Go away whatever you are!"

"I'm going to spin a web from your nose to the leg of the chair," said the spider. "Keep still!"

The lion gave a scream and ran away. He knew it was no use going to the ark. He knew it was no use going to the toy-cupboard either. Where could he go?

"What about the dolls' house?" he thought. "Yes, the door of that may not be locked!"

He ran to it. He pushed the front door. It opened! The lion slipped inside, shut the door and went into the kitchen. He sat down in a chair there and sighed. As last he was safe!

He didn't feel brave now. He didn't feel like a king. He just felt very small and lonely and frightened.

Katie found the lion in the dolls' house the next day, and how surprised she was! "How did he get there?" she wondered. "What a funny thing!"

She put him back into the ark. And that night, when the ark-animals clambered out of the ark, the lion went too, but he didn't go and sit on the hearth-rug alone, looking haughty and grand. No, he mixed with the others and played touch-me-last and hide-and-seek!

And when Mr Noah called the animals to him, who was the first one to come? Yes – the lion! He wasn't going to be locked out again! He had had enough of being grand and mighty. He just wanted to be a good little wooden animal now, ready to go into the ark with the others.

The lioness teases him sometimes. She says, "Who spent the night in the dolls' house like a doll?" And then the lion blushes red all over and doesn't say a word!

The Funny
Little Hedgehog

One morning when Dick looked out of the window he saw something on the lawn that made him look and look again.

"Mother," he said, "there's something in the bottom of the net that goes all round the tennis court. What can it be?"

Mother looked. There certainly did seem to be something rolled up in the bottom of the brown net. "Go and see what it is, Dick," she said. So Dick ran out into the sunshine. He came to the net and bent down. At first he couldn't see at all what was rolled up in it – and then, when he put down his hand to feel, something pricked him!

"Gosh! It's a hedgehog!" said Dick in

surprise. "Poor thing. It's caught in the net. I'd better undo it."

So Dick tried to undo the net from the hedgehog. The little prickly creature was very frightened and curled himself up tightly. Dick could not get him untangled from the net at all.

"Mother!" he called. "The prickles of the hedgehog are so tangled up in the net that I'll never be able to get him free. Shall I cut the net?"

"You'd better," said his mother. "But it is a pity, for it will quite spoil the net."

Dick fetched some scissors and gently cut away the net from the frightened hedgehog. How tightly he had curled himself up! Dick couldn't see his head or his feet – only lots of brown prickles.

At last the hedgehog was free from the net. He lay on the grass, still curled up.

"Mother, he's very frightened!" said Dick. "What can I do for him now? What will he eat?"

"Well, he usually eats beetles and grubs and things like that," said Mother. "But he will love a saucer of catfood, Dick. Go and get some from the kitchen."

"Oh, Mother! Perhaps the hedgehog will get tame and live in our garden for always," said Dick joyfully. "I should like that. I shall call him Spiky!"

Dick put a saucer of catfood down by the hedgehog – but the little creature wouldn't uncurl himself at all. He just lay there like a brown prickly ball, not moving.

65

Dick moved away and hid behind a bush. Soon he saw the hedgehog move. A tiny brown nose looked out – two black eyes gazed round – then, when the hedgehog thought there was no one about, he uncurled the whole of himself and stood on his four short legs.

He sniffed. Ah! What was that nice smell? Catfood – what a treat! In a flash the hedgehog had got his head and front paws into the saucer and was eating up the meaty food more

quickly than a cat.

Dick was pleased. It was fun to see a little wild animal behaving so tamely. The little boy made all sorts of plans. He would have him for a pet! He would teach him to come when he was called. What fun to see Spiky running up when his name was shouted!

But Spiky *wouldn't* be tame. As soon as Dick got near him he curled up tightly again. And when Dick left him to go to his dinner, Spiky hid himself so well that Dick couldn't find him at all afterwards. It was most disappointing.

But all the same the little hedgehog ate the tinned catfood that Dick put down each day. Dick couldn't think where Spiky had his home for he hardly ever saw him – and as the hedgehog came for his meal at night, he didn't see him feeding either.

Spiky lived in a cosy hole in the bank of the lane outside Dick's garden. There he had a fine home. In the winter he lined it with moss and dead

leaves to keep it warm, and slept there soundly, his head in his paws. In the summer he used it for a hiding-place and stayed there very often in the daytime, dozing. He liked his hole. He had been very frightened when he had run into the tennis net and got caught. No matter how he had struggled he hadn't been able to get free – he had only got more tightly into the net.

Dick soon forgot to worry because Spiky wouldn't be a pet. He put down the tinned catfood each evening – and then something happened that put the hedgehog quite out of his head. A burglar came to the house one night and stole the rings belonging to Dick's mother! Just fancy that!

He only had time to take three rings, because Daddy heard him, shouted at him, and frightened him. The robber jumped out of the window and ran away at top speed. Daddy ran after him and caught him. He called a policeman, and the robber was taken to prison – but will you believe it, when he got there he hadn't got those rings anywhere about him! His pockets were empty.

"He must have thrown them away as he ran," said the policeman. "We must hunt for them." So everyone hunted all round about – in the garden

– in the lane – and down the road to the police station. But nobody found them. They just didn't seem to be anywhere at all. The burglar wouldn't say a word about them. He just said, untruthfully, that he hadn't taken any rings.

"He's put them somewhere," said the policeman to Daddy. "And he means to go and get them some time or other when you've forgotten all about them."

"I do wonder where they are," said Daddy and Mother and Dick a hundred times a day.

Do you know where they were? They were in a most extraordinary place. As the burglar had run down the lane he had stuffed the three rings into a hole in the bank – and it was the hedgehog's hole! Spiky wasn't there – it was night-time, and he liked to go hunting for beetles and grubs then. The burglar felt sure no one would find the rings there. He meant to get them afterwards. Daddy hadn't seen him do this because it was a dark night. But there the rings were, stuffed into Spiky's hole!

Now Spiky didn't go back to his hole for two or three days. He had found a splendid place for slugs in a garden some way away, and was enjoying himself very much. He fed on fat slugs all night long and then, instead of going back to his hole, he curled himself up in a flower-pot and slept during the daytime.

When at last he did go back to his hole in the bank, one early summer morning, he was surprised to find something there that hadn't been there before. Three shining rings! They could not be eaten – they were too hard. Spiky didn't like them. He was afraid of strange things. He sniffed and sniffed and sniffed at the rings, and then crawled into his hole, trying to get behind them so that he need not touch them.

But the hole was small and Spiky had to lie on top of them. He didn't like it. He grew angry in his little hedgehog mind. He could not go to sleep because he was worried about the strange shining things in his hole.

"I'll push them out!" thought Spiky suddenly. "Of course! I'll push them out! I won't have them in. This is *my* hole! I won't have strange things walking in."

Just as he was about to push out the rings, he heard a noise of footsteps coming down the lane. He listened and heard Dick's voice, talking to his mother. Ah! He was not afraid of Dick. Spiky took a ring in his mouth and pushed aside the curtain of moss that hung over the entrance to the hole. He dropped the ring out. Then he went

back for the next one, and dropped
that out too.

And at that very moment Dick came
walking down the lane with his
mother. His sharp eyes caught sight of
something gleaming on the bank and
he gave a shout.

"Mother! Look! Is that one of your
rings? Oh! There are two!"

Even as Dick bent down to pick up
the rings, he saw the hedgehog's snout
poking out of the hole, and in Spiky's
mouth was the third ring. The
hedgehog dropped it and it rolled down

the bank. Then the curtain of moss fell over the entrance of the hole and Spiky disappeared.

"Mother! Oh Mother! Spiky had the rings in his hole!" shouted Dick. "And he waited until I passed by – and then he dropped them out for me. Oh, Mother, isn't he a wonderful hedgehog! I'm glad I was kind to him. I'm glad I rescued him from the tennis net and gave him food each night. He's paid me back for it, hasn't he?"

"Well, it certainly looks like it," said Mother, most astonished. She took her rings in delight. They were not a bit spoilt.

"To think they were in Spiky's hole all the time!" said Dick. "I expect the hedgehog found them and took them there to keep safely until he could give them to me, Mother."

"No, I don't think that," said Mother. "I expect the thief stuffed them into the hole, not knowing it belonged to a hedgehog who would throw them out."

"Good old Spiky!" shouted Dick, dancing round in delight. "I was a friend to you and now you're a friend to me. I wish I could take your photograph and send it to the newspapers. You ought to be famous."

But Spiky didn't like the sound of that. He disappeared from his hole when next Dick went to look for him, and now he is wandering about in someone else's garden. He may be in yours! Be kind to him, won't you!

The
Little Green Imp

The Prince of Ho-Ho had a very bad-tempered cook. None of the other servants liked her, but she was big and strong, and nobody dared to complain about her.

They had a very bad time until Twinkle, the kitchen-boy, came to work there. Mrs Pudding, the cook, made him get up at five o'clock in the morning, and would not let him go to bed until midnight, and the poor boy was working hard all the time.

But Twinkle had a grandmother who was half a witch, and when he got out one afternoon to go on an errand he ran to his grandmother's cottage in the wood.

"Granny!" he said, "tell me what to

do! There's a cook at the castle, and she gives me a dreadful time, and everyone else too! How can I stop her?"

His granny thought for a moment, and then she nodded her head. "Wait a minute!" she said. "I've just the thing for you!"

She took a big green dish and filled it full of water. She scattered a green powder into it and it changed the water to a brilliant emerald. She peeled a potato into it, stirred it round with a peacock's feather, and muttered words so magic that Twinkle felt a bit frightened.

"Watch!" said his granny. He looked into a bowl, and suddenly out of the green water there jumped a green imp

with a potato body and a grinning face!
He smacked his hands together and
looked up at Twinkle's grandmother.

"You'll do!" said the old lady, and she
laughed. "Here, Twinkle, put him into
your pocket. As soon as you get into the
kitchen, put him on a shelf and leave
him. He will do the rest!"

Twinkle thanked his grandmother
and put the green imp into his pocket.
The imp laughed out loud and pinched
him once or twice, but Twinkle didn't
mind. He guessed that imp would play
a few tricks on Mrs Pudding, the bad-
tempered cook!

As soon as he got into the kitchen he
put the imp on the shelf behind a
saucepan. Mrs Pudding turned round
and scolded Twinkle. "Why have you
been so long, you good-for-nothing
boy?"

"Now, Cookie, you be good!" said the
voice of the green imp suddenly from
the shelf. "Naughty, naughty,
naughty!"

Mrs Pudding turned round in a rage,

too astonished to speak. The green imp peeped at her from behind a saucepan and made a face.

"And what are *you* doing in my kitchen, I'd like to know!" said Mrs Pudding, her eyes gleaming with rage. "Come here!"

But that little imp stayed where he was, rapping out a tune on one of the saucepans, and grinning with all his might. "Oh, Cookie, what a naughty temper!" he shouted.

The other servants were all staring in delight and astonishment. How could that green imp dare to speak to Mrs Pudding like that? The cook went over to the shelf and put out her hand to get the imp, but he picked up a fork lying nearby and rapped her fingers hard. Then he pushed six saucepans on to the floor, one after another – bang! – crash! – smash! – bang! – crash! – smash! – what a dreadful noise they made! Mrs Pudding was very angry.

She picked up a newspaper and folded it so that she might hit the little imp with it. She brought it down on the shelf – bang! Two more saucepans and a kettle jumped off to the ground – bang! – crash! – clang! The imp was nowhere to be seen.

"That's finished *him!*" said Mrs Pudding, pleased. But, dear me, it hadn't. No, he had just jumped neatly off the shelf on to the kitchen table behind the cook. And on the table he saw a jug of milk. The imp grinned. He picked it up by the handle, jumped up on to the mantelpiece, and tilted the jug over Mrs Pudding's head.

Trickle, trickle, trickle! The milk fell on her head and ran down her neck! She got such a shock! How that imp laughed! He nearly fell off the mantelpiece with laughing. As for

Twinkle and the other servants, they roared too. But Mrs Pudding got angrier and angrier.

She picked up a large cabbage and flung it at the imp. He dodged it neatly and it hit the kitchen clock. Crash! Down came the clock and a big tea-caddy, and the cabbage too! The cook stared in horror!

"Oh, naughty, naughty, naughty!" said the imp, dancing about on the table again, on to which he had jumped again.

Mrs Pudding turned round to him,

and the wicked little thing threw an egg at her. It broke and went down her neck to join the milk. Oh dear – poor Mrs Pudding! What a sight she looked! The imp began to laugh so much that he was afraid he might be caught, so he jumped up on to another shelf and hid in a bucket there. Mrs Pudding looked all round for him, and when she could not find him she went to wash the egg off herself.

"How dare you all stand grinning there?" she cried to the other servants. "Get on with your work at once, and if you see that green imp anywhere about just catch him and bring him to me!"

But nobody meant to catch him. It was fun to see someone who was not

afraid of Mrs Pudding! She washed herself and then boxed Twinkle's ears for upsetting some salt.

"Oh, naughty Cookie, oh, naughty Cookie!" squealed the voice of the green imp, and he popped his head out of the bucket. Mrs Pudding saw him.

"Oh, so you've turned up again, have you?" she said. "Well, I'll get you this time!" And with that she took the bucket down from the shelf, but the imp hopped out and ran into the larder crying, "Can't catch *me*, can't catch *me!*"

Mrs Pudding rushed after him, but he was waiting for her. He threw a string of sausages round her neck and dropped a pat of butter neatly on her head from the top shelf. Really, you never knew what that wicked imp was going to do next!

All the evening things went on like that, and there was no catching that imp, and no stopping him either. Twice he emptied water over Mrs Pudding, and once he pelted her with apples he had found in a basket. Mrs Pudding rushed round and round the kitchen after him, but she couldn't seem to get hold of him at all. He was as slippery as an eel. He undid her shoe-laces when she wasn't looking. He undid her apron-strings and made her apron slip off a dozen times. He emptied pepper near her, and she sneezed thirty times

without stopping.

"Oh, won't someone get rid of this horrid little imp for me!" wept Mrs Pudding at last. "What has he come for?"

"I think he has come to tease you and torment you because you have treated *us* so badly," said Twinkle boldly.

"That's right, that's right, that's right!" squealed the imp from somewhere under the table, where he was busy untying Mrs Pudding's shoes again.

"If only you'd catch him and get rid of him for me I'd mend my ways and be better," sobbed Mrs Pudding, who was quite tired out.

"Very well, then, I'll try," said Twinkle, grinning to himself. He knew just what to do, for his granny had told him. He took a pat of butter, a dab of vinegar and a brown clove. He stuck the clove into the butter and smeared it with vinegar. Then he held it out to the imp.

The little green imp smelt the clove in the butter and came eagerly for it. Twinkle snatched him up and put him into his pocket.

"I'll go and give him to my old granny," he said to Mrs Pudding. "She will know what to do with him, for she is half a witch."

He ran off, chuckling to himself, and soon came to his grandmother's. When she heard his story, how she laughed! "That will cure her bad temper!" she said. "Tell Mrs Pudding that I will take the imp, but I shall not be able to keep him if she loses her temper again, for he will surely come back!"

So Twinkle left the green imp with

his granny, who set him to work polishing her kettles and saucepans until they shone. He was afraid to do anything cheeky to the old dame. She had made him from a potato, and she could turn him back into one again!

As for Mrs Pudding, she didn't dare to lose her temper again, for she was so afraid the imp would turn up in her kitchen once more. So now everything is peace and quiet there, and Twinkle the kitchen-boy is as happy as can be.

But he can't help wishing Mrs Pudding would lose her temper once or twice – it *would* be such fun to see that imp dodging about the kitchen shouting, "Naughty Cookie! naughty, naughty!" at the top of his cheeky little voice. I'd rather like to see him myself, wouldn't you?

The
Magic Rubber

Once upon a time Snooty the gnome found a most remarkable rubber. It lay on the ground, in the middle of the woodland path, a large, long rubber, pointed at one end, and round at the other.

"What a curious thing!" said Snooty, picking it up. "It must be magic. I wonder what it does."

He rubbed it idly against a young birch tree – and to his immense surprise the tree vanished!

"I've rubbed it out!" said Snooty in amazement. "Oooh! What a very magic rubber this is! It rubs things out!"

He went to a blackberry bush and rubbed the leaves with the rubber. They disappeared at once. Then Snooty rubbed a few toadstools with the strange rubber. They vanished too! How very astonishing!

"Hoo!" said Snooty, in delight. "This rubber will be very useful to me. I can think of a whole lot of things I'd like to rub out!"

Snooty put the rubber carefully into his pocket. Then he danced home, singing and whistling, for he was very pleased to think he had found such a wonderful thing.

He didn't tell anyone about the magic rubber. He meant to have a good time with it without anyone knowing! The first thing he did when he got home was to get out his best pair of shoes and rub a nail that was sticking up into the heel part. It always tore his sock – but now he could get rid of it!

Sure enough, the nail disappeared at once! The magic rubber rubbed it out! Snooty was pleased. He looked round to see what else he could rub out.

"Oh, yes," said Snooty, "I'll rub out the door between the kitchen and the hall. It's always swinging and banging, and I don't need it!"

So he rubbed the door out with his rubber! It was marvellous to see it go! It just went.

Then Snooty saw in his garden Whiskers, the black cat from old Dame Topknot next door. Now Snooty hated this cat because it sat on his flower-beds, and spat at him if he went near it. So he looked at it with a grin, and said "Ha! I'll rub you out, Whiskers!"

And out he went with the magic rubber – and do you know, he rubbed that black cat out! One minute Whiskers was there, and the next he wasn't! It was most extraordinary!

Snooty was delighted. What a fine rubber he had found! He looked over the high wall and saw that Dame Topknot had a plum-tree full of ripe plums. If only he could get some! He knew Dame Topknot was out, for he had seen her go by with her shopping-basket.

"I can't climb this high wall – but I can rub it out!" he said. "Good! I'll rub a neat hole in it, get through it, and take some of those plums before Dame Topknot gets back!"

So he rubbed part of the wall with the large rubber – and he rubbed so many bricks out that a big hole came. Snooty climbed through it and filled his pockets with plums! What a feast he would have!

Snooty had a good time with his magic rubber! He rubbed out a dog that came into his front garden. He rubbed out all the wasps that came sailing into his kitchen. He rubbed out a mess he made when he split a pail of dirty water over the floor! Dear me, the things he rubbed out!

And then Snooty did a very silly thing! The next day he heard a rat-tat at his door and he went to open it.

Outside was Mr Biscuit the baker, with his bill. Snooty hadn't paid Mr Biscuit for a very long time, and he owed him a lot of money. Mr Biscuit had come to ask for it. He walked into Snooty's kitchen and put his bill on the table.

"Will you please pay me for the bread and the cakes and the pies you have had?" he asked.

"I haven't any money at present," said Snooty. "I will pay you next week."

"That is what you always say!" said Mr Biscuit angrily. "I won't listen to you any longer!" And he banged his fist so hard on the wooden table that a teapot jumped off and fell on the ground – crash!

"You careless fellow, look what you've done!" shouted Snooty, in a rage.

"Pay me my bill and I'll give you fifty pence to buy a new teapot!" said Mr Biscuit, his long beard bristling.

"Never!" said Snooty. "Take yourself off, and take that dreadful beard with you!"

"It's a beautiful beard!" shouted Mr Biscuit.

"It ought to be cut off and made into a yard-broom for sweeping up rubbish!" cried Snooty rudely. And do you know what he did? He took out his rubber and rubbed out Mr Biscuit's beard! Mr Biscuit did look funny without it.

"What have you done?" he wept. "Oh, my beautiful, beautiful beard! It took me forty years to grow it!"

"Well, grow it again," said Snooty, "and grow your hair again too!"

He rubbed Mr Biscuit's hair – and that went as well! Mr Biscuit gave a squeal of fright and rushed out of Snooty's house. He ran down the street, weeping.

Everyone came out to see what was the matter, and when they heard how Snooty had rubbed out Mr Biscuit's beard and hair they were very angry.

"That is the magic rubber belonging to the Wizard Hurry-up," they said. "He will be very annoyed when he knows it has been used by Snooty. Let us go and tell him. No doubt that rubber has rubbed out Dame Topknot's cat, and made that hole in her wall, and rubbed out Gobo's dog too. Dear, dear, to think that Snooty might rub us all out if he wanted to!"

The Wizard Hurry-up was angry when he heard that Snooty had found

and used his rubber. He strode off at once to Snooty's cottage and banged so hard at the door that Snooty nearly jumped up to the ceiling with fright.

Snooty was too much afraid to open the door, but the wizard didn't wait – he just flung the door open and walked in.

"Where's my rubber?" he shouted to Snooty.

Snooty took it out of his pocket and gave it to Hurry-up without a word. Hurry-up took it and then rubbed it in three places on the ceiling and in four places on the walls. Big holes appeared!

"Other people can play about with a magic rubber too!" said Hurry-up. "But I don't expect you'll be pleased when the rain and the wind come through these holes, Snooty. Next time you find

stared and stared – for he knew that he had rubbed Whiskers out with his magic rubber.

And then he saw Gobo's dog in his front garden – and then he saw his kitchen door swinging and banging just as it used to before he rubbed it out!

Snooty ran to the Wizard Hurry-up and told him what had happened. "Everything has come back again," he said. "Did you know it would, Hurry-up?"

"Oh, yes," said Hurry-up grinning. "The magic lasts only a week – then whatever was rubbed out comes back again!"

"And would the bits of my roof and ceiling that you rubbed out have come back again too?" asked Snooty.

"Of course," said Hurry-up.

"And here I've been working hard all week long trying to mend those holes!" groaned Snooty. "What a waste of time and money – and how my poor back aches!"

"It serves you right!" said Hurry-up.

"You are very horrid," said Snooty.

"If you talk to me like that I'll get my rubber and rub you out!" said Hurry-up. "Now let me see, where did I put it – in this drawer, I think!"

But before Hurry-up could get his rubber, Snooty was gone. You couldn't see him for dust! He wasn't going to be rubbed out, not he!

Mr Biscuit's hair and beard came back again, and he went marching off to Snooty's with his bill once more. And Snooty paid it without a word. And how he has behaved himself since that week! He's always afraid Hurry-up will be after him to rub him out, you see!

99

"Right, Ma!" said Simon, and went back to his book.

Next day his aunt came to see his mother, who was out. The aunt sat down at the table and panted, for she was fat and the day was hot.

"Simon, get me some lemonade," she said. "I am so hot."

Simon went to the larder – but there was no lemonade.

"I'll make some for Aunt," thought Simon to himself. "I know how to – just lemons, sugar and hot water! Ho, won't Aunt think me clever!"

He got the lemons and the sugar. Then he looked round for something to put the lemonade in.

"Let me see, what did Ma say?" he wondered. "She said next time I was to use the WATERING-CAN! Right! I'll get it! Oh, I'm a clever boy, I am!"

He got the big watering-can, first emptying out some soot-water his mother had put there for watering her pot-plants. Then he squeezed the lemons into the can, added the sugar and poured hot water on to the top. He stirred the can several times, and then heard his aunt calling him.

"Simon, Simon, whatever are you doing? Are you growing the lemons for the lemonade, or what?"

"Coming, Aunt, coming!" called Simon. He ran into the kitchen and put a glass in front of his aunt. Then he fetched the big watering-can, and lifted it up – but the sprinkler was on the end of the spout, and instead of pouring the lemonade into the glass, he sprinkled it all over his aunt's best dress!

He ran into the kitchen and took down a small cream-jug. Then out he went again to the tree. He picked some ripe plums and popped them into the jug – but the jug was small, and would take only three plums. Simon looked at it and frowned. Then a good idea came to him.

"Well, I'll take the stones out and that will make a bit more room."

So he tore open the ripe plums and picked out the stones. Then he crammed the pulpy mess into the jug. He managed to get about ten plums in, but that was all. He squashed the mess down, and hurried in to his mother.

"Have you got me those plums yet?" said his mother impatiently. "Or are you waiting for next year's fruit, Simon?"

"No, Ma!" beamed Simon. "Here you are!"

He handed his mother the jug and she looked into it in disgust.

"What is this dreadful mess you've got in here?" she asked. "Is it squashed beetles or something?"

"No, Ma, it's the plums!" said Simon. "I tried my best to get you twenty, but the jug wouldn't hold them even if I took the stones out."

"What! You've squashed plums into that cream-jug!" cried his mother. "What will you do next, Simon? Have you no brains? Really, I think you must have a potato instead of a head! Empty out that dreadful mess whilst I go and pick some plums. And do remember this – next time use a BASKET! Yes, a BASKET!"

107

"Ooh!" said Simon. "Where is it?"

"There it is!" said his father, giving Simon a good smack. "Look! There's a trail of it all over the yard! Why don't you *think*, Simon? Fancy putting sand into a *basket!* Next time, use a TIN!"

"Oh," said Simon, and then went off to his dinner, for his mother was calling him.

The next week his aunt came to say that she had a dear little puppy that Simon might like to have for his own if he liked.

"You can fetch it this afternoon," she said. Simon was simply delighted. But before he went, he stood and thought for a moment.

"Now what shall I take to bring it back in?" he wondered. "What did Pa say to me? Yes, I remember – he said 'next time, use a TIN'!"

So Simon went to the shed and found a large tin with a lid. He set it on his shoulder and went off to his aunt's. She was doing her washing.

"The puppy is somewhere around the yard," she said. "Go and get it, Simon – and see that you treat it well!"

Simon soon found the puppy, which came running to him. He lifted it up and put it into the tin. He put on the lid, and set off home.

But the puppy did not like being in the tin. It whined and pushed at the lid with its head. It soon pushed it off, and Simon had hard work to carry the tin and to put the lid on, too, whenever the

straightway set out for his aunt's house, and I don't blame it! So Simon didn't have the pup after all.

It wasn't long before Simon was sent on an errand again; this time was to fetch an umbrella that his mother had lent to Dame Flippy. He set off, whistling, and soon reached Dame Flippy's house. She gave him the umbrella and a lollipop.

"Now you be careful how you take this umbrella home," she said to Simon, who was sucking his lollipop. "It's your Ma's best one, so just you be sensible!"

Simon went down the street thinking. What was it his ma had said to him last time he went on an errand? Oh, yes – next time use a STRING! Well, that would be easy. He had a nice long piece in his pocket. It would be less trouble to drag a piece of string behind him than to carry a large umbrella on such a hot day!

So Simon tied his string to the handle of the umbrella, and then dragged it

along behind him through the dust. He pretended that he was a galloping horse, that the umbrella was his driver, and the string his reins. He galloped up and down, shouting at the top of his voice, and soon arrived home.

"Well, Simon, you haven't been long," said his mother. "But where is my umbrella?"

Simon looked at the end of his string. The umbrella was not there! The string had broken and the umbrella had been left behind.

"Simon! Do you mean to tell me that you *dared* to drag my best umbrella through the streets at the end of that bit of string!" cried his mother. "Oh, you naughty, wicked boy. Come here!"

But Simon knew better than to come here! He darted off down the road again, to find the umbrella. He did find it, and took it home, pleased with himself – but when his mother saw the torn, dirty, bent thing that had once been her very best umbrella – well, I really cannot tell you how angry she was!

"It's no better than a stick now!" she cried. "I can't use it at all!"

Simon's mother raised the umbrella above her head, but Simon didn't wait to see if she'd use it! It didn't take him long to rush out of the house, I can tell you! And whether he is still a potato-head or not, I haven't heard. But I'll tell you when I know!

The Tale
of the Goldfish

Once upon a time, thousands of years
ago, there lived in China a merchant
who was very fond of fishes. He kept
four big ponds, and in each swam a
different kind of fish, some little, some
big, some brightly-coloured and some
speckled with silver spots. The
merchant loved his fish and fed them
every day.

He liked his bright-coloured fish the
best. There were some that had blue
streaks down their sides, and others
that seemed to have caught a rainbow
in their tails. The merchant leaned
over his ponds to watch his fish and
longed for one thing – to breed a fish
that was bright gold from nose to tail!

"There are plenty of silver fish!" he

said to himself. "There are many rainbow-coloured fish, and others that are spotted and speckled with brilliance. But no one in the whole world has ever had a fish that was all gold. How lovely it would be! How everyone would marvel! There could never be a prettier fish than a gold one, and it would give pleasure to all people, no matter where they lived."

So he tried very hard to rear a fish that was all gold. But he found it was impossible. Some fish had bright yellow spots on them. Some had orange-coloured streaks; but none was all gold from tip to tail.

The merchant fell on bad times. He lost a great deal of his money, and became poor and shabby. He shut up his large house and lived in a small corner of it, without servants to wait on him. But he did not forget to feed his fish. He became an old man, and gave up the idea of rearing a fish of gold. He found that he was happy even though he was poor, and when his little grandchildren came to see him and climbed on his knees to listen to his stories he wished for nothing better.

One night a strange traveller came to the old merchant's house. The great bell outside the gate jangled to and fro as it had not done for years, and the merchant heard it in surprise. Who could be coming to his house now? He had no rich friends; they had all forsaken him.

He went through the long passages that led to the front gate and unbarred it. Outside stood a cloaked man, his horse beside him.

"Does Wong Fu, the great merchant, live here?" asked the visitor in a deep voice.

"Honourable sir, it is Wong Fu you see before you," said the merchant, bowing, "but I am no longer great. I am

119

a poor man, and my house is empty. Enter, I pray you, for I will find you shelter and food, though it will not be of grand quality."

The visitor stepped inside. The merchant took him to a great marble basin where he might wash, and then slipped out to see to the horse. He stabled it in the empty stable, gave it food to eat and then went to prepare a meal for his unexpected guest.

In an old chest he had a few dainties stored away, and these he took out. Soon he had a meal ready and went to call his visitor. He found him leaning over the ponds, looking at the fish in the moonlight.

"You are fond of your fish, I see," said the visitor, raising his head. "They come swimming up to my hand, tame and friendly."

"Yes," said the merchant. "It has always been the dream of my life to breed a fish all gold from head to tail – but I have never done so. Come, honourable sir, your supper is prepared."

They sat down to eat, and at last the visitor told the old merchant who he was and why he had come.

"I am Sing Fu," he said, "the son of the old washerwoman you had many years ago."

"But you are a wealthy man, well-favoured and wise," said the old merchant in astonishment.

"It is so," said the visitor. "My mother put me in the service of Lai Tu the famous magician, and I found favour in his sight so that he made me like a son to him. Now Lai Tu is dead, and I have his wealth and much of his learning."

The merchant got up and bowed himself to the ground, until his forehead touched the floor. He was in great awe of enchanters, and he trembled to think that he had one in his shabby house.

"Rise," said the visitor. "Do not kneel to me. My mother would not have you do that."

"And is your honourable mother still alive and well?" asked the merchant, seating himself again, but still trembling in his surprise and excitement.

"She is well and happy," said the enchanter, gravely. "It is by her

122

request that I have come to see you. Do you remember her, honourable host?"

"Yes," said the merchant at once. "She was fat and jolly. She washed my linen better than anyone else."

"And do you remember when she fell ill and could not work for five weeks?" asked the visitor.

The merchant felt uncomfortable. Had he treated the old washerwoman kindly? He could not remember. It would be dreadful if she had sent her son to punish him for an unkindness done to her years ago.

"No, I do not remember her illness," he said at last.

"My mother remembers," said the magician. "You picked her up and carried her up to bed. You sent a doctor to make her well again, and you paid her wages all the weeks that she could not work. She has never forgotten. And now that she has a son who is wealthy and powerful she has asked me to go to all those who were once kind to her and reward them. So I have come to you."

The old merchant was amazed.

"And do you also visit those who treated your mother ill?" he asked. "Do you punish as well as reward?"

"No, for such is not my mother's wish," said the enchanter, gravely. "She has forgotten her enemies, but not her well-doers. Now, honourable friend, you are poor and shabby. I bring you riches and honour, and they will bring you happiness."

"There you are wrong," said the merchant, quietly. "Neither riches nor honour bring happiness. I am happy now, without them. I do not want gold, nor do I want servants, rich food, embroidered clothes. I am old and tired, but I am happy. Leave me as I am."

The magician looked at the old man in wonder. Never before had he met anyone who refused what he had to offer. He said nothing more, and, bidding the merchant good night, lay down on a mat to sleep.

But in the middle of the night he went to his horse and took a sack from its back. In this sack were great bars of gold, which he had brought as a present for the old man. Now they would not be wanted. But the magician had thought of something splendid to do with them.

He took them to one of the ponds, where pretty grey-green fish were swimming, and one by one he slid the bars of gold into the water, murmuring magic words as he did so. Each bar dissolved into a cloud of orange-gold,

and behold, the fishes were attracted by the strange mist in the water and swam up in shoals to see what it was.

And when morning came, each fish was bright orange-gold from head to tail! The old merchant saw them when searching for his midnight visitor, who had strangely disappeared. He stood by the pond, amazed and delighted. His dream had come true at last! Here were goldfish – bright gold from nose to tail!

And when you see a gleaming goldfish, remember the kind-hearted merchant and his old washerwoman, and be kind to others yourself. You never know what magic you may start!

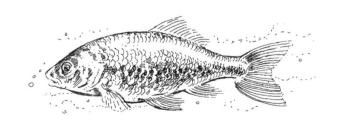

Winkle
Makes a Mistake

Winkle was a mean and dishonest old gnome. If he found a bad coin he pretended it was a good one and gave it to a shopkeeper on a dark evening. If he could borrow anything and not return it, he did. His house was quite full of basins, brooms and plates he had borrowed and never taken back!

"You'll be sorry one day!" said the people who knew him. "Yes, you will! People like you don't get on well in this world!"

But Winkle only grinned – for he really got on very well indeed. He had a long red stocking put away full of money. He always had chicken every Saturday for dinner, which his black cat caught for him from the farm over

the hill, and he always had warm clothes to wear in winter.

"I get on all right!" he said to himself. "What's the sense of being honest if it keeps you poor? No, no – I'll go my own way and be rich!"

So he went on being mean and dishonest, and getting richer and richer.

Now one day he went shopping in the next town. He bought all kinds of things, and asked the shops to send them home to him. The only parcel he took home was a brown paper one with his mended shoes inside.

He caught the bus and sat down. Next to him was a very smart fellow, a gnome who lived in a big castle in the

next village to Winkle. He took no notice of Winkle at all, although the gnome said "Good morning." He didn't like the look of Winkle, it was plain.

Winkle got out at his village, picked up the brown paper parcel and walked home, feeling very cross with the fine gnome who hadn't said "Good morning" to him. He put down his parcel and put on the kettle to boil.

After he had had a cup of cocoa and some bread and cheese he opened his parcel to take out his mended old shoes – and what a surprise he got!

In the parcel was a pair of very fine shoes indeed – oh, very fine ones, fit for a king to wear! They were of leather sewn with gold, and had gold laces

threaded through, and buckles set with pearls. Winkle stared at them in astonishment.

"The old cobbler at the shop has put the wrong shoes in my parcel!" he thought to himself. "Silly old fellow! How careless of him! Well, I'm not going to bother to give them back to him. He shouldn't have been so silly as to make that mistake! I shall keep them and wear them! Ho, ho!"

Wasn't he mean? He ought to have taken them back at once to the cobbler, of course. He put them away in his cupboard and longed for a party so that he might wear them and be very grand indeed.

Now it wasn't the cobbler who had

made the mistake at all. He had put the right shoes in the gnome's parcel – Winkle's old mended ones. It was *Winkle* who had made a mistake – for in the bus he had sat next to the smart gnome who had also a parcel with him; and in *his* parcel was a pair of very fine shoes he had been to buy for His Majesty the King! Winkle hadn't looked to see that he was taking the right parcel when he jumped from the bus – he had picked up the parcel belonging to the other gnome and gone off with that.

So when the grand gnome arrived home and opened *his* parcel, what should he find but a pair of old mended shoes and he was most disgusted. He guessed at once what had happened. The other gnome in the bus, the one who had said "Good morning" to him, must have taken the wrong parcel. Oh, well, it was annoying, but no doubt when the other fellow found out his mistake he would bring back the shoes.

But, of course, Winkle didn't. As you know, he put them into his cupboard and kept them for himself, thinking that the cobbler had made a mistake.

Now when the grand gnome didn't get the shoes brought back, and found that nobody had asked the bus conductor about them, he decided to put up notices everywhere, to say what had happened, and to tell the gnome who had taken the wrong parcel where to bring the shoes. So he wrote some notices in red ink and stuck them up all over the place, in the villages around.

At the top of the notice he printed three words very large indeed. The words were "GOLD-LACED SHOES". Anyone catching sight of those words and having the wrong shoes at home would be sure to read the notice, thought the grand gnome, and he would soon have the shoes back.

Well, it wasn't long before Winkle the gnome did see those notices, and read the words at the top: "GOLD-LACED SHOES". But he didn't read any

further.

"It's only that silly old cobbler putting up notices about the shoes he gave me in mistake for my own," thought Winkle. "Well, if I don't read the notice, I can't find out anything more about the grand shoes, and as I don't *want* to find out anything, I shan't read the notice!"

So he didn't – and he was the only person in the village who didn't know that the shoes belonged to the King himself!

Well, when no one brought back the shoes to the grand gnome in his castle he became angry.

"Someone is keeping them for himself!" he thought. "Oho! Well, I can soon stop that! Shoes, come to me, and clatter as you come!"

Then a most extraordinary thing happened. Those gold-laced shoes, put safely away in Winkle's cupboard, began to struggle to get out. They wriggled out of the door and began to make a clatter on the floor. Winkle heard them and ran to see what was the matter.

When he saw that the shoes were trying to get away he was surprised and angry and put them back into the cupboard again.

But once more they struggled out, almost breaking the door down! They wriggled away from Winkle's hands and danced downstairs. They shot out of the front door with Winkle after them and clattered off down the street, making a great noise.

"Stop! Come back!" yelled Winkle, who wasn't going to lose those fine shoes if he could help it. But the shoes took no notice at all. They just went on, making a great clatter all the way down the street. Then people poured out of

their houses to see the strange sight, and followed Winkle and the shoes, laughing and pointing. What an excitement for the village! Wherever were those shoes going?

The shoes went clattering to the next village and climbed up the steps of the castle where the grand gnome lived. He heard them coming and went to meet them. He saw behind them an angry gnome, trying in vain to catch hold of the dancing shoes.

"Take this man," the big gnome ordered his servants. "Bring him before me in my castle."

He picked up the shoes, and strode inside, the servants following with the surprised Winkle between them. Winkle was truly amazed. Why was he suddenly treated like this?

He stood before the grand gnome.

"How come you have these shoes?" asked the gnome sternly.

"Oh – the c-c-cobbler put them into my parcel by m-m-mistake," stammered Winkle, in fright.

"Why didn't you take them back to him, then?" said the gnome.

"Well, if he was silly enough to make a mistake I thought he should be punished for it," said Winkle, more boldly.

"I see," said the gnome. "You think if people make mistakes they deserve to be punished, even if they didn't mean to make them?"

"Certainly," said Winkle.

"Well, listen to a little tale I have to tell of a gnome who made a big mistake," said the grand gnome, in a

137

stern voice. "Once there were two gnomes in a bus, each with a brown-paper parcel. One gnome had old mended shoes in his parcel, but the other had gold-laced shoes he had bought for His Majesty the King. Now one of the gnomes got off the bus first and by mistake took the wrong parcel."

Winkle grew pale. How dreadful! So it wasn't the cobbler's mistake after all – it was *he*, Winkle, who had made a mistake!

"As you have just said," went on the grand gnome, "a mistake must be punished, even though it was not made on purpose! You will go to prison, or pay a fine of one hundred pounds to the poor people of the villages around! Oh, Winkle, you think I have not heard of

you and your mean, dishonest ways – but your name is known by everyone! You are rich – but only by wrong-doing! Now you shall be poor, and also by wrong-doing! Well – which is it to be – prison or one hundred pounds?"

"I haven't got one hundred pounds," wailed Winkle. "I've only seventy in my long red stocking at home."

"Bring me that," said the gnome. "And work hard and honestly for the rest, which you must bring to me as you earn it. And remember this, Winkle – riches got by ill means will sooner or later fly away, even as yours have done! Now go!"

Winkle stumbled home, sobbing and crying, to fetch his hoard of money. He was bitterly ashamed of himself. His neighbours pointed at him and nodded their heads.

"We told him so!" they whispered to one another. "Meanness and dishonesty only come to one end!"

Poor Winkle! He is working hard every day now. His hoard of money is gone, and he is trying to earn more to make up the hundred pounds. But he has learnt his lesson. If he borrows, he pays back. If he finds what isn't his, he gives it back to the owner at once. He doesn't cheat, he doesn't shirk. And it may be that by the time he has earned enough money to pay the hundred pounds, he will be a different person – straight, honest and true.

I hope so, don't you?

What a Surprise!

Barry was very fond of birds, and every morning he put out crumbs for them, and a saucer of fresh water. He made a bird-table, too – just a piece of wood on the top of a pole – and from it he hung strings of unshelled peanuts which he had carefully threaded together, and a coconut with a hole made at each end. He put all kinds of tit-bits on the table, and you should have seen the birds that came to visit it!

When Barry's birthday came, the postman knocked at the door and left three parcels, a small one and two big ones. Inside the small one was a silver pencil – and inside the two big ones were wooden nesting-boxes to put up in the garden for the birds to nest in!

Barry was so pleased.

"Just what I've always wanted!" he said, looking at the two boxes in delight. They were very nicely made, and the top part, which made a slanting roof, could be lifted up – so that Barry would be able to peep inside and see if any bird had begun to nest there.

"I shall put these nesting-boxes up today," said the little boy. "I shall put one in the chestnut tree – I know a fine place there – and one I shall fasten among the rose ramblers. There is such a small hole in each for the birds to get in and out that I am sure only the tiny tits will make their homes there. What fun it will be!"

So out he went very happily into the garden, and soon the two nesting-boxes were in their places. One was well hidden among the ramblers and the other was neatly hung on the trunk of a small chestnut tree, protected by an overhanging branch.

"If I were you, Barry," said his mother, "I would hang up bits of fat or

peanuts near your new nesting-boxes, and then, when the tits come to them, they will see the boxes and perhaps think they are good nesting-places."

So Barry hung a few peanuts by each box, and begged a piece of suet to hang up too. In ten minutes' time the tits had found the nuts and the suet, and were very busily pecking away at them. Barry could hear them calling to one another in excitement.

"This is suet, this is, this is suet, this is! Peanuts, peanuts, peanuts! This is suet!"

The tits were pleased to find more food in the garden. They thought that Barry was the nicest, kindest boy in the world, and they were always happy in his garden. One of them flew to the top of a nesting-box. He wondered what it was – it hadn't been there before. He hopped about all over it, sometimes the right way up, sometimes upside down. He didn't really mind whether he swung one way or another!

Then he called to his wife, "Come and see!"

She flew down to him. "Look!" said the tit in excitement. "There is a little hole here. It leads into a nice dark room. Let us go inside and see whether it would be a good place to nest in."

So in they went, and they both decided that it would be exactly right. This was the box that Barry had put in the rose ramblers. The other box was taken by another pair of excited tits, who were most delighted to find such a fine nesting-place.

"It's near plenty of food!" they sang. "It's in the garden of the nicest boy in the world! There are no cats! We shall be safe, safe, safe!"

Then they began to build their cosy nests. They made them of the softest things they could find – bits of moss taken from the ditch, a great many hairs from the post against which the brown horses in the field rubbed themselves each day! And some hairs from the dog next door. When he shook himself a few hairs flew from his coat, and the tits were always on the watch

for these. They would hunt about the lawn for them.

Then they lined their nests with soft feathers. Some they found in the hen-run, and how they squabbled with the sparrows over them! The sparrows liked the feathers too, to make a lining for their nests, and tried their best to take them all – but the tits pounced down in a flash, and carried off most of the downy feathers under the very beaks of the angry sparrows!

146

The nest of the tits in the rose rambler box was finished first. It was so cosy and warm. Barry knew that they were building there, for he watched them carrying moss and hair in their beaks to the ramblers. He was delighted. One day, when he knew that both the tits had left the nest, he went quietly to it and lifted up the roof-lid. He gazed inside before he shut down the lid, and to his great delight saw five pretty little eggs. Now there would be crowds of fluffy yellow baby tits calling all over the garden to their parents!

He ran indoors to tell his mother.

"I'm so glad," she said. "But if I were you, Barry, I wouldn't peep inside any more. The tits may not like it, and it would be so dreadful if you made them desert their nest and leave their eggs or young ones. It does sometimes happen, you know."

147

So Barry did not go and peep any more. When he did the next time he got a great surprise, as you will hear.

Now, as you probably know, all birds and animals can see the little folk, although very few humans can do so. The tits especially are friendly with them, for the fairies love the merry, pretty little birds, with their bright voices and amusing ways.

Very often the tits went to the woods nearby where many elves lived, and in their hunt for small insects they came across many of the little folk and talked to them. And one day the tits that nested in the rose rambler box found an elf of great use to them.

She lived in a hole at the foot of an old oak tree. The two tits often went to hunt for insects in the bark and the elf liked their merry voices, and always popped her little golden head out to wish them good day.

One morning the tits were hunting in the oak tree bark when a gun went off not far away. It was the farmer shooting rabbits. It frightened the tits so much that they rose straight up into the air to fly – and one of them flew full-tilt into the branch overhead and hurt himself so badly that he fell down to the ground in a faint, his eyes closed, and his wings drooping.

"What's the matter, what's the matter?" called his little wife, in a fright. She flew down to her mate, but he did not move. Then she heard a scampering of feet not far off and saw

the bright-eyed weasel, whom all small creatures and birds fear, for he feasts on them.

"Help! Help!" cried the little tit, in a panic, and she flew up into the air. The weasel stopped – and then came running over to the oak tree.

But before he could snap up the poor little tit someone came rushing out of the roots of the oak. It was the golden-headed elf. She caught up the tiny tit and ran back with him into her home. He was safe there, for the weasel could not possibly squeeze into the small hole where she lived.

"I'll pay you out for that!" he shouted at her and ran off, mad with rage, for he was hungry.

In a few minutes the tit opened his eyes and stretched his wings, none the worse for his bump. When he found the elf bending over him, and heard what had happened, he was very grateful indeed.

"It is most kind of you!" he said, in his shrill little voice. "Most kind indeed! Let me know, elf, if you want help yourself at any time, and my wife and I will be very pleased to do whatever we can for you!"

Then he flew with his wife, back to his nest in the box, where he rested all day and was soon quite himself again. When their eggs hatched out into five pretty little youngsters, the two tits were mad with delight. They sang about them until everyone in the garden was quite tired of hearing how beautiful and how marvellous the baby tits were. But indeed they really were very sweet, for they were just bundles of blue and yellow fluff.

One day the robin brought a message to the two tits.

"Blue-tits!" he sang, "I bring a message to you from the elf in the woods. She is very unhappy and asks you to go to her."

Off went the tits at once. The elf was not in her usual place under the oak tree – but they found her shivering in the ditch not far away, with only a cobweb shawl wrapped round her.

"What is wrong?" cried the tits, flying down beside her.

"Oh, little friends," said the elf, "a

dreadful thing has happened to me. The weasel was so angry because I saved the life of one of you the other day that he said he would force me to go away. He sent an army of red ants into my cosy home and they ate up all my pretty clothes, and bit me so hard that I could not stay there any more. Now they are building their nest in the oak tree roots, so I have no home. I don't know where to go, because if I choose another hole the ants will come after me there too. Now, here I am, cold and hungry in this ditch, with only this cobweb shawl to keep me warm. I am so dreadfully afraid that the weasel will come after me."

"You poor little thing!" cried the tits, cuddling close to her. "What can we do for you? Let us think hard!"

So they thought very hard, and then the little hen tit cried out in delight.

"I know! I know! Let the elf come to live with us in our nesting-box! It is true that we are rather crowded now that we have five babies – but it is warm and cosy, and the elf will have plenty of company and be quite safe from the weasel there!"

"Oh, that would be wonderful!" said the elf, tears of joy coming into her eyes. "Oh, there is nothing in the world that I would like better! I could look after the babies for you when you went out together, couldn't I!"

"Yes, you could!" cried both tits,

delighted. "There is one of our children who is far too bold. We are afraid he will climb out of the little entrance hole one day and fall to the ground. Then the weasel will be sure to get him. If *you* were living in the nest with us we should never be afraid of leaving the babies alone. Do come!"

The elf spread her pretty gleaming wings, and flew up into the air with the

tits. The weasel, who was hiding in the bushes not far off, gave a snicker of rage. He had been hoping to pounce on the elf that very day.

The tits took the elf to their nesting-box. She was just too big to squeeze in through the little hole, so she had to lift up the roof and get in that way. She cuddled down among the fluffy babies and was soon as warm as toast.

How happy she was there! And how pleased all the seven tits were to have her! She was so good to them all. She looked after the five babies carefully when the two parents were away, and wouldn't let the bold one try to climb out of the hole. She saw that each baby had his share of the food in turn, and would not let the strong ones rob the weak ones. She brushed their feathers and told them tales. They loved her very much indeed.

She was very warm and cosy there, and had plenty to eat, for the little tits brought her all kinds of food each day. They knew which flowers had the sweetest honey, and they were very clever at bringing leaves with dewdrops on them, so that the elf could drink. Nobody knew that the elf lived in the box, not even the other tits. It was a secret.

And then somebody found out. Guess who it was! Yes, it was Barry. He did so badly want to see how many baby birds the tits had in the rose rambler box. So one sunny morning he tiptoed to it, after he had seen the tit parents fly out, and he lifted up the roof-lid to see inside.

He looked down – and there, looking up at him, were five fluffy blue and yellow baby tits – and one pretty, golden-headed elf! She was cuddled down among the tits, her arms round them, the prettiest sight you could imagine!

Barry was so surprised that he simply stood and stared. Then he quietly shut down the lid and went away. It was the greatest and loveliest surprise of his life – a real secret that he couldn't tell anyone at all.

When the parent birds came back, the elf told them what had happened. She was frightened. "I must fly off!" she said. "That boy will come back and take me away."

"No, no," sang the tits at once. "Don't be afraid of Barry. He is the nicest boy in the world! He would not harm us, and he will not harm you. You are quite safe here. Let him peep at you if he wants to. He will never, never hurt you!"

When the five baby tits flew away into the garden in the bright summer-time, the elf stayed in the nesting-box and made it her home. She tidied it up, and she made a small cupboard for herself and a shelf where she put all her belongings.

"Do come back and nest here next

year," she begged the tits, who often came and peeped in at the hole to talk to her.

"We will!" they promised. "We certainly will!"

So there the elf still lives, as Barry knows very well! He peeps at her once a week, and she knows him well now and smiles gaily at him. He has never told anyone his great secret – but I know because the tits told the robin and he sang it all to me! And how I'd love to go and peep in that box – wouldn't you?

The Cow that Lost Her Moo

There was once a pretty cow called Buttercup. Everyone was very fond of her, for she was a gentle creature, though rather stupid. She lived in a big field with twelve other cows, and she was the prettiest of the lot.

One day she caught a cold and she lost her voice. She tried her hardest to moo loudly just as she had always done – but it wasn't any good at all. Not the tiniest bit of moo came out of her big mouth. Buttercup had no voice except a small whisper that sounded rather like dry leaves rustling together.

"This will never do!" thought Buttercup to herself in a great fright. "I *must* get some sort of voice. I can't go about whispering. Even the ducks on the pond over there have a louder voice that I have. If I can't moo perhaps I can learn to quack!"

So that night, when the Little Folk came running out in the fields, Buttercup whispered to one of them.

"Pinkity, I've lost my lovely moo. Could you get me another one, do you think? – or at any rate could you get me another voice of some sort? I hate talking in a whisper like this; it is so stupid for a large cow like me to have such a tiny whispery voice."

Pinkity looked at the large cow and grinned all over his cheeky little face. "I can't get you a moo," he said. "But I could get you a quack, if you like! I know those ducks would spare me one if I asked them."

Buttercup nodded her head. Off went Pinkity, spoke to the ducks, and then came back with something wrapped up in a dock leaf. "Here you are," he said to the grateful cow. "Swallow this and you'll find you have a fine new voice!"

So Buttercup swallowed down the dock leaf with the quack spell inside – and at once she found that she could quack!

You should have heard her! Really, it was funny to hear a big cow quacking away for all she was worth. Her friends came round her in surprise.

"Why do you quack?" they asked. "You are very foolish, Buttercup. The farmer will think you are a duck, and will put you on the pond to swim with the others. You will have to lay eggs for him."

"Quack, quack!" cried Buttercup, in a great fright. "I couldn't lay an egg! I know I couldn't! And I should die of fear if I had to swim on the pond!

163

Pinkity, where are you? Quack, quack, quack! Take away this quack and bring me some other voice. I can't bear it!"

Pinkity hopped up. He was very much enjoying himself. He caught a loud quack as Buttercup spoke, and wrapped it up in another dock leaf. He put it into this pocket, and hurried off. He went to a brown mouse for a little squeak. She gave it to him wrapped up in a daisy leaf, for it was very small.

He ran back to Buttercup and gave it to her. She swallowed it – and then began to squeak in a very high voice, just like the mouse. All the other cows began to moo with laughter.

"Buttercup, how foolish you are!" they said. "Now you have a voice like a mouse. The weasel will come along when he hears you, and will try to bite you, thinking you are a mouse – and the big owl will pounce down on you."

"Too-whoo-too-whoo!" called the owl, in the distance. Buttercup began to tremble. She was in a great fright.

"Pinkity, Pinkity!" she squeaked. "Come here! Take away this squeak, I beg of you, and bring me a better voice. I can't bear this. Squeak, squeak. Eeeeeeee!"

Pinkity took away the squeak and ran off again, beaming.

This was a great joke. What a tale to tell when he went home in the morning!

This time he went to a sheep lying down on the hillside, and asked her to lend him her baa. She did so, and he carried it off, wrapped up in two nettle leaves. Buttercup swallowed it gratefully and at once began to baa and bleat in a most sheep-like manner.

All her friends stared at her in amazement. Whatever would she do next?

"Buttercup, are you turning into a sheep?" asked Daisy, a pretty white cow.

"No," said Buttercup. "Of course not. I am a cow. Baa-aa! Baa-aa!"

"Well, the farmer will be sure to think you are a sheep if you baa like that," said Daisy. "He will expect you to grow wool for him and will clip your coat just as he does those of the sheep. My! You will be cold with all your coat clipped away!"

Buttercup was horrified. What! Have her nice hairy coat clipped away so that she might grow a thick covering of wool? Never! "Baa, baa, baa!" she bleated to Pinkity. "Oh, do take this voice away quickly. I can't bear it.

Baa, baa!"

Pinkity hopped up and took it away. He gave it back to the surprised sheep, and then hunted round for someone else who might lend him a voice. He met Bobby, the dog, out rabbiting by himself in the moonlight, and he called to him.

"Hey, Bobby! Will you lend me your bark for a little while?"

"No," said Bobby. "I want it."

"Now, listen, Bobby," said Pinkity. "I'll show you the best rabbit hole in the field if you'll lend me your bark for a time. Please do. I'm having such fun with a foolish cow. I've made her quack, squeak and baa. Now I want to make her bark."

167

"Well, mine's a very *fierce* sort of bark," said Bobby. "She will frighten all the other cows if they hear it. So I warn you, Pinkity ... you'd really better not borrow it!"

But Pinkity said yes, he really must have it. So Bobby gave it to him, wrapped up in a piece of paper he found in the ditch. Off went Pinkity over the fields to Buttercup. "Here you are," he said, giving her the bark in the piece of paper. She ate it up, paper and all.

And then, stars and moon! She began to bark like a very fierce dog!

"Wuff, wuff, wuff! Grrrrrrrrr! Wuff, wuff, wuff, wuff! GRRRRRRRRRRRR!"

There had been a growl mixed up with the bark, and so Buttercup growled as well as barked. The other

cows, who all disliked and feared dogs, were terrified almost out of their lives. They rushed off to the other end of the field in a fright.

As for Buttercup, she was terribly frightened too! She hated dogs, and this bark and growl she had made her very much afraid. She galloped away – and trod so heavily on Pinkity's toes that he yelled with pain. He limped off crying big tears down his cheeky little face, and went home to bathe his poor foot.

So when Buttercup went to find him to beg him to take her bark away, he was nowhere to be seen! No – he was safely at home, tying up his poor squashed toes in a bandage, wishing very much that he hadn't played such silly tricks on foolish Buttercup!

Buttercup barked all through the night, and growled when she wasn't barking. Her friends were so frightened of her that they wouldn't let her come near them.

"If you come any nearer we will run our horns into you!" they cried. "You are turning into a dog, there's no doubt! You will have to live in a kennel and eat biscuits and bones, instead of sweet grass."

Buttercup was very unhappy. She went away into a corner and barked all to herself. "Why did I bother about my voice?" she thought sadly. "I would rather have no moo at all than bark like a dog. This is dreadful. What will the

farmer say when he milks me?"

The farmer was scared and puzzled when he heard Buttercup's new voice. He stared at her as if he couldn't believe his ears. A cow barking? What next?

"Wuff, wuff!" said Buttercup, hanging her head in shame. "Wuff, grrrrr!"

"I shall have to sell you, Buttercup," said the farmer, seeing how frightened of her all the other cows seemed to be. "I can't have a barking cow."

"Wuff, grrr!" said Buttercup, most unhappily. She couldn't bear the thought of being sold. It would be dreadful to leave the fields she knew and go somewhere strange.

All that day she barked and growled, and when night came she looked out anxiously for Pinkity. That rascally little creature had been feeling sorry that he had played such tricks on Buttercup. His toes were very painful, and he thought it must be a punishment for him.

"I'd better go out and see how Buttercup is tonight," he thought to himself. "Even though I can hardly walk, I must certainly go."

So out he went into the field. No sooner had he gone through the gate than he almost jumped out of his skin. He heard what seemed to him to be a very fierce dog barking and growling just above him. Of course, it was Buttercup waiting for him. What a fright he got!

"Wuff, wuff, grrrrr!" said Buttercup. "Do pray take this terrible voice away, Pinkity. Wuff! I frighten everyone and myself too. I would rather have no voice at all. It was foolish of me to want one."

Pinkity took the bark and growl away and wrapped them carefully in his handkerchief. Then he limped off to find Bobby, who, he was sure, would be wanting his bark badly.

So he was. He was very angry indeed about it!

"You said you only wanted my bark for a little while!" he scolded. "Here I've had to be all day without either my bark or my growl and couldn't even bark at an old tramp who came and

173

stole some eggs. So I got a beating for not doing my duty. Give me my bark at once!"

Pinkity gave it to him – and then forgot all about his bad foot, for angry old Bobby chased him up the lane and over the fields, barking at the top of his voice!

"Wuff! You mischievous creature! Grrrr! You scamp, you rogue! Wuff, grrr, wuff!"

Buttercup was very thankful indeed to have lost her bark. She ate grass quietly, and when her friends saw that she no longer barked or growled they came round her once again and talked to her.

And suddenly she found herself mooing to them! Yes – her cold had gone away, and she had got her own voice back once more! It had gone only for a little while whilst she had a cold. So she needn't have worried herself so much after all!

"To think I had a quack, a squeak, a baa, a bark and a growl!" said

Buttercup to herself, in shame. "When all the time, if only I'd been patient, my own voice was just waiting to come back. Really, I am a very foolish cow! I do hope the farmer won't sell me now."

He didn't, of course. When he found that Buttercup was her own self again, and mooed just as she always did, he patted her and said: "Well, well – I can't think what happened to you yesterday, Buttercup – but you seem all right today, so, as you give me a nice lot of creamy milk, I shan't sell you!"

"Moo, moo, moo!" said Buttercup, and whisked her tail happily. Then she whisked it again and knocked off the farmer's hat. But he didn't seem to mind!

Miss
Mary Ann Mouse

There was once a small brown mouse with long black whiskers and a neat tail. She was called Mary Ann, and she lived with her mother and father and brothers and sisters in a hole behind the attic wall.

Her family were very untidy. They used bits of chewed-up newspaper for a bed, and they left bits of cheese, bacon-rind and crumbs all over the floor. Mary Ann didn't like it. She was a tidy little mouse, and hated to see messes and muddles.

She made herself a little broom and swept up the hole three times a day. She cleared up the bits of newspaper and put them neatly at one side until bedtime. She wished she could find little plates to make the family eat from, but she couldn't.

Now you might have thought that her family would be pleased to have a tidy little mouse putting everything neatly in its place – but they were not!

"Where's my bit of cheese gone that I saved for my dinner?" cried Whiskers in a rage. "Mary Ann, have you swept it up?"

"Where's my bed gone? I want to have a nap!" squealed Mrs Mouse. "Mary Ann, you surely haven't put it away! Get it out at once."

"I want my bit of bacon-rind – I want my bit of bacon-rind!" squeaked little Tailer-Mouse, the baby. "Mary Ann, where have you put it?"

"I slipped and fell on it this morning, so I swept it up, Tailer," said Mary Ann. "I'm so sorry."

"Mary Ann, you are a perfect little nuisance!" said her mother. "Go away!"

"Mary Ann, we don't want you, always tidying up and interfering," cried all her brothers and sisters, and they took her by the whiskers and threw her out of their hole.

Poor Mary Ann! She sat outside the hole and trembled. She was afraid of cats, and she knew there were two in the house. But she dared not go home again. She knew she would only be thrown out of the hole once more. She was much, much too clean and tidy for her mouse family.

"Nobody wants a tidy mouse," thought Mary Ann sadly. "Nobody at all. Whatever shall I do!"

She ran quietly to the door. She sat there and woffled her nose, sniffing hard to smell if either of the cats was about. But she couldn't smell one. She

ran into the next room. This was a boxroom, and into it had been put all the old things that were not wanted downstairs.

There were big and little trunks there, piled in one corner. There was a broken chair, and an old stool stood nearby. Unwanted pictures stood with their faces to the wall. And in one corner stood an old dolls' house, belonging to the little girl of the house.

But the little girl was no longer a little girl. She was growing up and she didn't play with her dolls' house. Her mother had made her nursery into a bedroom, and the dolls' house, with its furniture and family of dolls, had been put into the boxroom and forgotten.

Mary Ann, the little mouse, saw it there and looked at it. It *did* look a nice place! It had a front door with a knocker that badly wanted cleaning. It had curtains at the windows which badly wanted washing. Mary Ann crept over to it and pressed her little woffly nose to one of the windows. Nobody seemed to be there, inside the house. And, oh, how Mary Ann shivered with delight to see the dear little beds, and the kitchen with its saucepans and kettles!

"But how dirty it all is!" said Mary Ann to herself. "I'll find out who lives there." But she couldn't find out because there was no one to ask.

She turned the handle of the front door – and it opened. Inside was a dark little hall, very dusty and dirty. A door opened off one side to the kitchen and on the other side to the living-room.

The little mouse had a look round. Then she ran upstairs. There were four bedrooms there, one a very tiny one indeed that had just room for a cot and a washstand and that was all.

"How happy I should be if I could have this little room for my own," thought the mouse. The cot just fitted her. She curled herself up in it for a moment.

Now the doll family who lived in the house had gone away for a holiday. There was Mrs Tiny, the mother doll, and Mr Tiny, the father doll, and five small girl and boy dolls called Alice, Bertie, Annie, Davey, and Lucy. Mrs Tiny had such a lot to do, looking after

the house and the cooking and the five children, that she had fallen ill, and Mr Tiny had taken the whole family away to his brother's for a holiday. This was why the dolls' house was empty; but Mary Ann didn't know this of course.

The little mouse fell asleep, curled up in the cot. When she awoke she sat up in a hurry. Suppose someone had come and found her asleep in their house? She jumped out of the cot and ran downstairs. But there was no one there at all.

"I'd love to tidy up the house a bit," thought Mary Ann, rolling up her sleeves. She found a check apron in a

182

drawer in the kitchen and put it on. She thought it would be fun to light the kitchen fire. So she did, and soon there was a nice cheerful blaze in the little kitchen.

Well, then you should have seen Mary Ann! She found a brush and dustpan and swept all the carpets. She took down the curtains and put them to soak in soapy water. She polished all the boards of the floor and made the furniture so bright with rubbing that she could see her little whiskery face in every table. She scrubbed the kitchen floor. She polished the taps in the bathroom until they shone. She folded

up all the untidy clothes left on the floor and chairs and put them away in cupboards and drawers. She had a perfectly lovely time.

At last she sat down and made herself a pot of tea. She sat by the kitchen fire, her nose going up and down in delight, for she was very happy. If only, only she had a house like this to keep tidy and clean!

"It doesn't seem to belong to anyone, so I shall enjoy myself keeping it nice each day," thought Mary Ann, sipping her hot tea. "Tomorrow I shall wash the blankets. The next day I shall clean the stairs down. The next day I shall beat all the carpets. What fun I shall have!"

Mary Ann did have a lovely time the next few days. Soon the dolls' house began to look as clean and beautiful as it had looked on the day that it had been new. The door-knocker shone and winked in the sunshine that came through the boxroom window. The windows were as clean and clear as could be, and the curtains were snowy-white. Everything in the kitchen shone and glittered, and the bedrooms were beautiful.

One day Mary Ann looked round the house and really couldn't find a single thing more to do. "I think I'll see if that stove in the kitchen cooks well," she thought happily. "I'll make some buns!"

So she bustled about and made some beautiful buns with currants in – and they turned out just right. Mary Ann was very pleased. She felt tired when she had finished, so she set the buns on the kitchen table to cool and ran upstairs to tidy herself and have a little rest.

And, do you know, just as she got into her cot and fell asleep, the doll family came home! Yes, Mrs Tiny and Mr Tiny and all the children.

"Oh!" groaned Mrs Tiny as they drew near their home. "I'm not looking forward to getting home – everything will be so dirty and untidy – there will be such a lot of work to do!"

But when she got to the front door, what a surprise she got! The knocker shone and winked! The paint was freshly cleaned! Mrs Tiny opened the door. The hall was tidy and smelt of polish! She went into the living-room.

Everything there was spick-and-span and shining.

"What does this mean?" cried Mrs Tiny in amazement. "Is this my house? Look at those curtains! They are snowy-white! Someone has washed them. And look at the furniture shining – someone has polished it."

"Mother, the kettle and saucepans in the kitchen are so bright we can hardly look at them!" said Alice.

"Mother, the kitchen floor has been scrubbed and it does look lovely!" said Bertie.

"Oh, Mother, Mother, there are some lovely currant-buns on the kitchen table!" cried Annie excitedly. "Can I have one?"

Mrs Tiny went into the kitchen and stared at the buns in astonishment.

187

She couldn't understand it at all. She went upstairs and looked into the bedrooms. The beds were neatly made – the blankets had all been washed – everything was spick-and-span and tidy as could be.

All this time Mary Ann was fast asleep in the little cot. Davey and Lucy, the two youngest dolls, peeped into the little bedroom – and they saw Mary Ann in the cot.

"Mother! Mother! There is a mouse in the cot we used to sleep in!" cried Lucy, half frightened.

Mrs Tiny went in to see – and there was Mary Ann, waking up, very startled to see a family of small, strange dolls

looking at her.

Mr Tiny spoke first. "What are you doing in our house?" he asked sternly.

Mary Ann began to cry. "I didn't know it was your house," she said. "I thought it was such a dear little house and I just came in and cleaned it well. It was so dirty and untidy."

"Mother, I like this little mouse," said Alice, and she felt Mary Ann's woffly nose.

"Mother, did this mouse make those currant buns?" asked Bertie. "I want one."

"Madam, you look tired," said Mary Ann, scrambling out of the cot. "Just you go off and take off your things now, and let me get tea for all of you. The beds are all aired and quite clean, and the kitchen fire is going, so the water will be hot for the children's baths. I wont be a minute."

Well, in ten minutes Mary Ann had made tea and laid the table in the living-room. She had put two plates of her new buns there, and whilst the doll

family were eating them, she sped upstairs and unpacked all the luggage. She got the children's beds ready and then ran the water in the bathroom for their baths.

And do you know, little Mary Ann Mouse bathed all those children one by one and got them into bed as good as gold. She told them marvellous stories of her life in the mousehole, and they listened in delight. They thought she was a most wonderful mouse.

When the children were asleep and everything was cleared up, Mary Ann Mouse tidied herself, gave a big sigh, and went into the living-room where Mr and Mrs Tiny were sitting talking.

"I've come to say goodbye, madam," she said. "I'm sorry I lived in your house without you knowing – but I did so enjoy cleaning it. Now I will go back to my mousehole."

"Oh, no, you won't, dear little Mary Ann!" said Mrs Tiny. "You'll stay with us. I want someone who can help me and love the children. If you like living in a house and having a little cot for a bed, stay with us. We will love you and treat you well, and you shall do all the cleaning and tidying you want."

Well, you should have seen Mary Ann's nose go up and down for joy! It went so fast that Mrs Tiny could hardly see it. Mary Ann picked up her tail and danced round two or three times in delight.

"I shall love to stay," she said. "I will keep house for you, and love all the children. This is just what I always wanted."

And there she is to this day, little Mary Ann Mouse, scurrying about the dolls' house in the boxroom, making the beds, scrubbing the floors, bathing the children, as happy as the day is long.

The greatest treat she has is to dress the children in their outdoor clothes and take them for a walk out of the boxroom into the attic next door to show them the mousehole where her family live. And how all her brothers and sisters stare when they see Mary Ann peeping in with Alice, Bertie, Annie, Davey, and Lucy!

192